Mom Is Single

Words by Lena Paris

Pictures by Mark Christianson

 CHILDRENS PRESS, CHICAGO

6 7 8 9 10 11 12 R 93 92 91 90 89 88 87

Library of Congress Cataloging in Publication Data

Paris, Lena.
    Mom is single.

    SUMMARY: A young boy describes some of the good and
bad aspects of living with his single working mother.
    [1. Single-parent family—Fiction.   2. Mothers—
Employment—Fiction.   3. Mothers and sons—Fiction]
I. Christianson, Mark.   II. Title.
PZ7.P2175Mo   [Fic]   79-22585
ISBN 0-516-01477-3

Mom Is Single

Today Mrs. Phillips, our teacher, told us that we would be making something special for parents' night. She said we could use the whole blackboard to draw a picture in colored chalk.

Then Mrs. Phillips told us that we were going to make name tags for our parents to wear on parents' night. She passed out little white cards.

Everyone else was excited about having their parents come to the classroom. But I just felt sad. It seemed like everyone had two names to put down except me.

I wanted to put Dad's name down and pretend that he would be there. But I know he has to work that night. When I got the cards, I put down Marie Shaw. That's my mom's name. I didn't write anything on the other one.

Writing Mom's name on the card made me think about Dad. I started thinking about the way things used to be when Dad was part of our family. Things sure have changed since Mom and Dad got a divorce. Now Mom and Dad don't want to be together at all.

When I leave school I wait for my sister Julie. Instead of going home we walk over to Mrs. Mayer's house. Mom said we can't stay home alone. So we stay at Mrs. Mayer's until Mom is through with work.

Mrs. Mayer lives in our neighborhood. She's real nice. At first I didn't want to stay at someone else's house. I wanted to go home after school. I wanted Mom to be there like she used to be when Dad lived with us. Mom said she would like to be there to meet us, but there wasn't anything she could do about it. It just wasn't possible anymore. It's better staying at Mrs. Mayer's than coming home to an empty house.

Before Mom got a job, she went back to school. She said that she had to go back so she could get a better job and help support us. Mom said even with her job, we would have to stay on a budget. At first I wasn't sure what a budget was. It sounded like some kind of diet. But instead of being careful of the food you eat, you are careful of how you spend your money.

Now I know how a budget really works. It means on your birthday you get clothes instead of a football. I would rather have the football.

Something else has changed too. Now when we get home, we all have jobs to do. We even have a job list. This week I have to set the table and dry the dishes. Julie has to clear the table after we eat. She has to take out the garbage too.

I don't always want to help. Sometimes I get angry. Why did things have to change? Mom said that without Dad, things had to change. We would be doing new things. She would be doing some of the things that we used to depend on Dad to do.

I thought we had to learn how to do things because Mom might leave too. Or maybe something might happen to her. I told Mom how I felt. She talked with Grandma and Grandpa. They said if anything ever happened they would take care of us. That made me feel a lot better.

Now Mom, Julie, and I wash the car, clean up the yard, and even paint together. I did some of those things before. But I used to do them with Dad. The birdhouse we built together is still in the backyard.

Dad and I still do things together. But it's not like before. Now Dad lives in another part of the city. He has a special room at his apartment for Julie and me when we visit.

Sometimes Julie and I do the same things with Dad that we do with Mom. We wash the car or go shopping or even visit the zoo.

I miss Dad the most right after he brings us home. He doesn't like to come in the house, so he waits near the car till we get in the door. He says he misses us too. But I wonder if he's as lonely as I am when he waves good-bye.

I used to think about Dad all the time when he first left. Now Grandpa and I do some of the things Dad and I used to do together. Sometimes we go fishing or to a ball game. But Grandpa doesn't always have time to do things with me. And he can't do some of the things Dad and I used to do.

Last week there was a camp-out. All my friends were going with their fathers. I asked Dad if he would go, but he said he had other plans. Grandpa said he was too old to sleep out in a tent. I felt terrible. Then Uncle Kenny said he would go with me. It was neat. We went boating and built a fire every night.

I used to pretend Mom and Dad would get back together again. Now I know they won't. But just because they don't want to be together doesn't mean they don't care about Julie and me. It just means things are different. It doesn't mean that things are better than before or worse. They're just different.